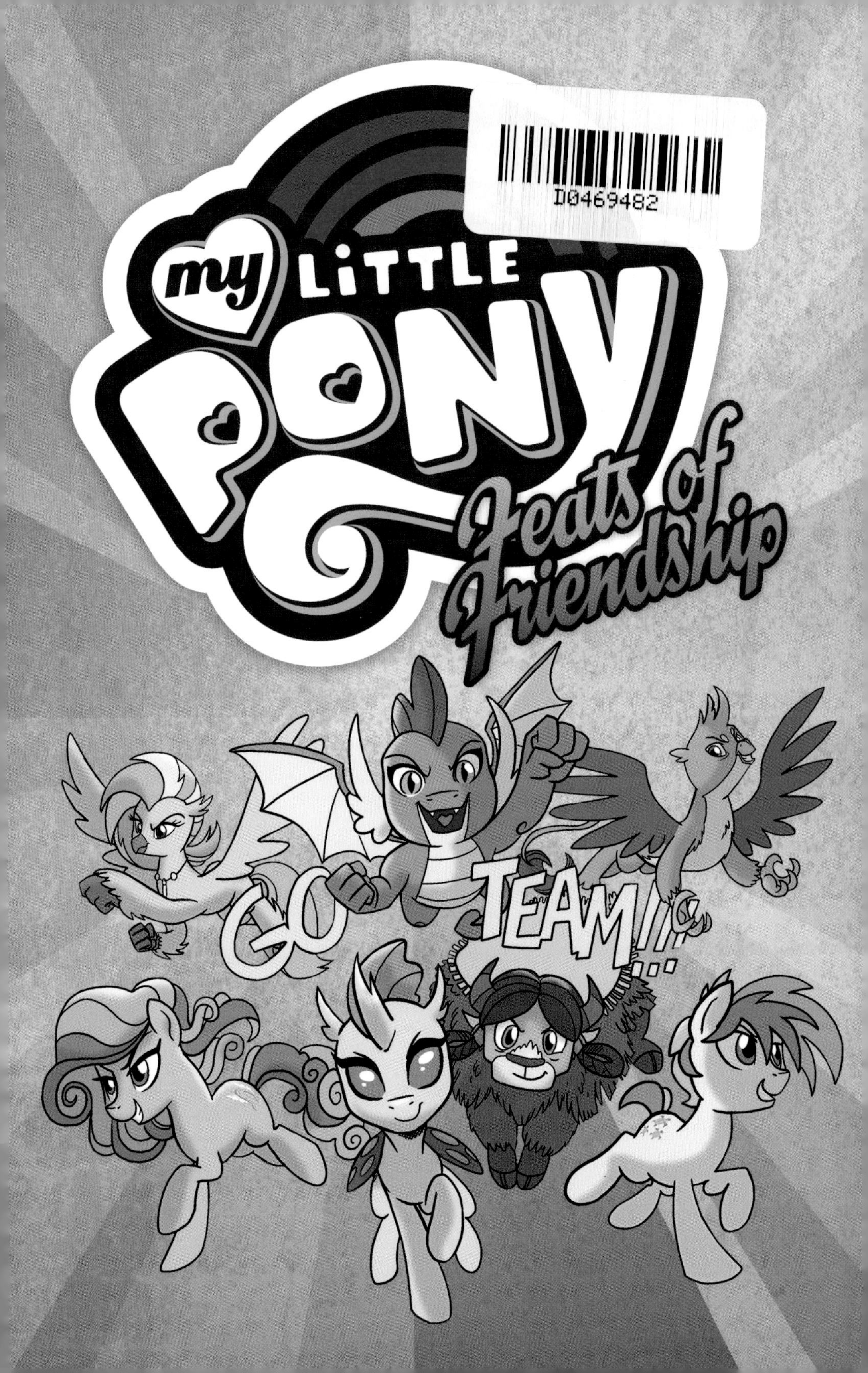

D0469482
my LITTLE PONY
Feats of Friendship
GO TEAM!!!

IDW

Facebook: facebook.com/idwpublishing
Twitter: @idwpublishing
YouTube: youtube.com/idwpublishing
Tumblr: tumblr.idwpublishing.com
Instagram: instagram.com/idwpublishing

Cover Artist
TONY FLEECS

Series Editor
MEGAN BROWN

Group Editor
BOBBY CURNOW

Collection Editors
ALONZO SIMON
and ZAC BOONE

Collection Designer
CHRISTA MIESNER

ISBN: 978-1-68405-671-2 23 22 21 20 1 2 3 4

MY LITTLE PONY: FEATS OF FRIENDSHIP. JUNE 2020. FIRST PRINTING.
HASBRO and its logo, MY LITTLE PONY, and all related characters are trademarks of Hasbro and are used with permission. © 2020 Hasbro. All Rights Reserved. IDW Publishing, a division of Idea and Design Works, LLC. The IDW logo is registered in the U.S. Patent and Trademark Office. IDW Publishing, a division of Idea and Design Works, LLC. Editorial offices: 2765 Truxtun Road, San Diego, CA 92106. Any similarities to persons living or dead are purely coincidental. With the exception of artwork used for review purposes, none of the contents of this publication may be reprinted without the permission of Idea and Design Works, LLC.

Printed in Korea.

IDW Publishing does not read or accept unsolicited submissions of ideas, stories, or artwork.

Originally published as MY LITTLE PONY: FEATS OF FRIENDSHIP issues #1–3.

Licensed By:

Hasbro

Special thanks to Tayla Reo, Ed Lane, Beth Artale, and Michael Kelly.

Chris Ryall, President & Publisher/CCO
Cara Morrison, Chief Financial Officer
Matthew Ruzicka, Chief Accounting Officer
David Hedgecock, Associate Publisher
John Barber, Editor-In-Chief
Justin Eisinger, Editorial Director, Graphic Novels & Collections
Scott Dunbier, Director, Special Projects
Jerry Bennington, VP of New Product Development
Lorelei Bunjes, VP of Technology & Information Services
Jud Meyers, Sales Director
Anna Morrow, Marketing Director
Tara McCrillis, Director of Design & Production
Mike Ford, Director of Operations
Shauna Monteforte, Manufacturing Operations Director
Rebekah Cahalin, General Manager

Ted Adams and Robbie Robbins, IDW Founders

Written by
Ian Flynn
Art by
Tony Fleecs
Color Flats (part 1) by
Lauren Perry
Colors (part 2-3) by
Heather Breckel
Letters by
Christa Miesner
and Neil Uyetake

LIKES

Swimming, stairs, indoor plumbing, art, school, going out, having fun, hanging with friends, literally everything ohmygosh—

DISLIKES

The Storm King.

LIKES

Helping my friends, hanging out with my friends, going to school with my friends—oh, and plants!

DISLIKES

Nothing, dude!

LIKES

Winning and gems. No, there's nothing else. No, I don't like cute things, I don't know where you'd get that idea, I totally do not like dressing up, nope—!

DISLIKES

Not winning. And fighting with my friends, I guess. Did I mention not winning?

LIKES

Teasing and playing pranks

& FRIENDSHIP!

DISLIKES

Classical music and ~~friendship~~.

LIKES

Um, um—studying, learning, and meditation.

DISLIKES

Public speaking! Oh, gosh, I can't even think about it!

LIKES

Yakyakistan, all things yak, sharing all things yak with great friends, also all of Yona's friends!

DISLIKES

Used to hate spiders, until one day Yona realize they only want to be friends! Yona loves friends!

AMF!
19
Art By
Tony Fleecs

"THE SCHOOL OF FRIENDSHIP WAS ESTABLISHED TO SPREAD THE WISDOM AND BENEFITS OF FRIENDSHIP...
"NOT JUST TO EVERYPONY, BUT TO ALL CREATURES ACROSS EQUESTRIA.

"TO REINFORCE THIS, WE'RE ORGANIZING THE FIRST FEATS OF FRIENDSHIP!
"A SERIES OF TEAM-ORIENTED CONTESTS THAT WILL CHALLENGE THE STUDENTS TO APPLY THE LESSONS THEY'VE LEARNED TO REAL-WORLD EVENTS."

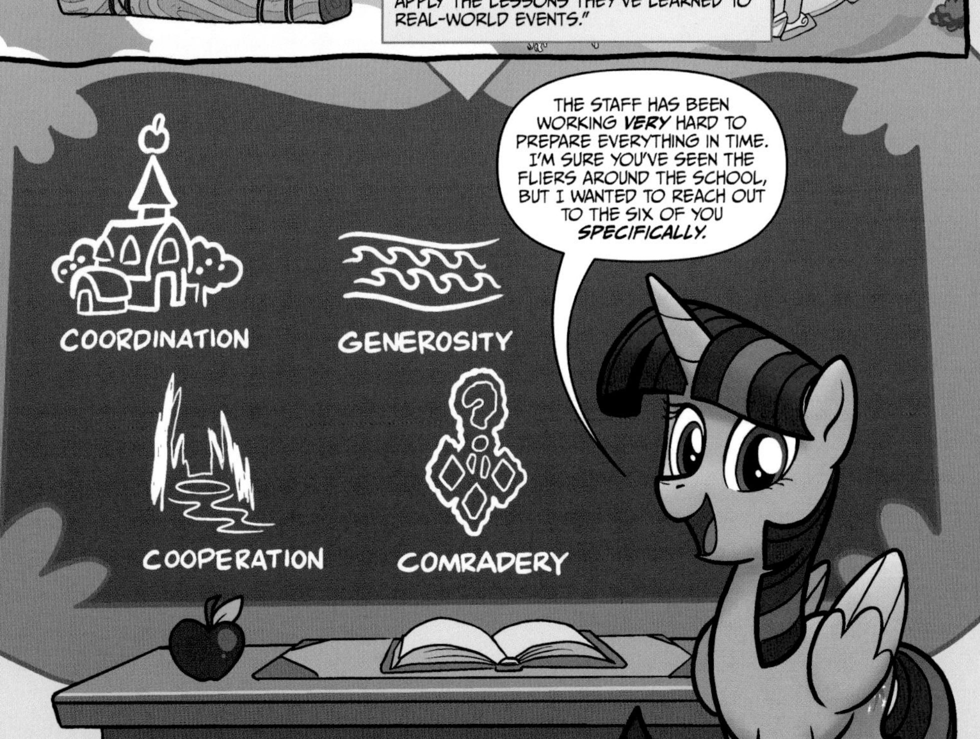
THE STAFF HAS BEEN WORKING VERY HARD TO PREPARE EVERYTHING IN TIME. I'M SURE YOU'VE SEEN THE FLIERS AROUND THE SCHOOL, BUT I WANTED TO REACH OUT TO THE SIX OF YOU SPECIFICALLY.
COORDINATION
GENEROSITY
COOPERATION
COMRADERY

SO... WE'RE NOT IN TROUBLE.
NOT IN THE TRADITIONAL SENSE, BUT...
WE ALREADY SIGNED UP AS A TEAM! SO WHAT CAN WE DO FOR YOU, MADAM PRINCIPAL?
I SAW YOUR FORM, BUT THE RULES CALL FOR SEVEN TEAM MEMBERS. I WAS HOPING YOU'D CONSIDER ADDING OUR NEWEST TRANSFER STUDENT, SWIFT FOOT.
HELLO...
YES!
I MEAN, LIKE, TOTALLY.
WE'D BE HAPPY TO HAVE HER.
REALLY? YOU'LL LET ME JOIN YOU JUST LIKE THAT?
TOLD YA.
THE SEVEN OF YOU WILL BE EMBODYING EVERYTHING THIS SCHOOL IS ABOUT. I EXPECT GREAT THINGS FROM YOU.
ALSO, IF YOU'D LIKE TO EARN EXTRA CREDIT, WE COULD USE SOME HELP IN FINISHING PREPARING FOR THE FEATS.
NO WORRIES, MA'AM. WE'VE GOT THIS.

WHY DID I SAY THAT?
YEAH. THANKS FOR VOLUNTEERING FOR US.
"EMBODY EVERYTHING THIS SCHOOL IS ABOUT"?! THANKS FOR THE PRESSURE!

EEE! IT'S FINE! I'M *SO* EXCITED! I GET TO EXPERIENCE SOMETHING IN PONY CULTURE FOR THE FIRST TIME—BECAUSE IT IS THE FIRST TIME!
YONA CAN'T WAIT TO WIN ALL THE THINGS WITH FRIENDS!

PLUS WE GET TO SEE THE FEATS BEFOREHAND! ISN'T THAT EXCITING?

RIGHT, SANDBAR?
SANDBAR?
SO, LIKE, TRANSFER STUDENT, RIGHT? RIGHTEOUS.
HAHA, IF YOU SAY SO.

YONA TRANSFER, TOO!
YOU DON'T SAY?
YONA DO SAY! SUPPOSED TO GO TO YAKADEMY UNTIL COME HERE!
WHUD
YOU SEEM TO HAVE COME FROM ALL OVER.
YEP. STRAIGHT OUT OF THE DRAGON LANDS.
EH, GRIFFONSTONE ISN'T *THAT* EXOTIC.
I'M FROM THE CHANGELING KINGDOM.

AND YONA FROM YAKYAKISTAN!
HAHA! I ASSUMED AS MUCH.

ARE YOU FROM OUT OF TOWN, TOO?
NAWI'MFROMM ARONERE...

TO TRANSLATE FROM MUSH-MOUTH: NO, HE'S A LOCAL.

WHERE IS NEW FRIEND SWIFT FOOT FROM?
UM...
OH... IT'S NOWHERE YOU'VE HEARD OF, I'M SURE. JUST ANOTHER SUNNY LITTLE PONY VILLAGE.
YOU KNOW... THE USUAL...
OHMYGOSH YOU GUYS! WE'RE BEING SO RUDE! WE HAVEN'T EVEN INTRODUCED OURSELVES TO OUR NEW TEAMMATE!
HI! I'M SILVERSTREAM, AND I'M FROM SEAQUESTRIA!
RIGHT. I'M SMOLDER.
MY NAME IS OCELLUS!
GALLUS.
AND THIS IS MUMBLES.
SNBRR...

NO! SANDBAR! I'M SANDBAR!

TOO LOUD? AW, MAN, TOO LOUD...

AND YONA IS YONA!
I'LL KEEP THAT IN MIND.

OKAY! WE'RE ALL INTRODUCED AND WHATEVER. CAN WE GET TO THE EXTRA CREDIT WORK SO WE CAN BE DONE WITH IT?
OOOH! THE FEATS ARE ALL OVER THE PLACE!

OKAY, THEN I GUESS WE SHOULD SPLIT UP. WE CAN MEET UP AT THE END OF THE DAY.
WHAT ABOUT SWIFT FOOT? SHOULDN'T ONE OF US SHOW HER AROUND THE SCHOOL?

WHY NOT BOTH? YOU ALL DO WHAT YOU THINK IS BEST, AND I CAN BOUNCE AROUND BETWEEN YOU.
THAT WAY I CAN LEARN MY WAY AROUND TOWN, AND I'M NOT SLOWING ANY OF YOU DOWN!

STRAIGHT TO THE POINT. I *LIKE* YOU.

AND YOU CAN GET TO KNOW US ALL AT THE SAME TIME! YEE! THIS IS GONNA BE GREAT! WE'LL WIN THE FEATS *FOR SURE!*
THANK YOU! ALL OF YOU!

I CAN'T WAIT TO GET CLOSER TO EACH OF YOU.

SOON...
...AND UP **HERE** YOU CAN SEE CLEAR ACROSS PONYVILLE!
IT'S A LOVELY CAMPUS.

YEAH, IT IS! BUT FOR ME, NOTHING COMPARES TO SEAQUESTRIA. **OR** MOUNT ARIS FOR THAT MATTER!
THAT'S RIGHT—THE HIPPOGRIFFS WERE FORCED TO LIVE UNDER THE SEA BY THE... **STORM KING,** WASN'T IT?

YUP! BUT NOW THE STORM KING IS GONE, AND WE'RE FREE! AND NOW I'M AT THIS AWESOME SCHOOL!
THAT'S... GREAT, REALLY.

YOU SOUND LIKE YOU'RE DISAPPOINTED?
OH! NO-NO-NO! IT'S JUST...
...IT WAS OUR TEACHERS WHO MADE THE JOURNEY AND STOPPED HIS EVIL, RIGHT?

ISN'T IT JUST... **WEIRD** THEY DIDN'T LIFT A HOOF UNTIL HE THREATENED THEIR KINGDOM?
OH... YEAH, I GUESS...

I MEAN... THEY DIDN'T KNOW... RIGHT?
I'M NOT SURE HOW THEY MISSED IT. A WHOLE KINGDOM—A WHOLE *RACE*—JUST VANISHING LIKE THAT...
AND YOU CAN'T REALLY *QUESTION* THEIR INTENTIONS, CAN YOU? THEY'RE *HEROES.* THEY'RE OUR *TEACHERS.*
I BET YOUR FRIENDS PRACTICALLY WORSHIP THEM, LET ALONE EVERYONE ELSE.
BUT WHAT DO I KNOW? I'M NOT FROM AROUND HERE.
ANYWAY, THANKS FOR THE TOUR! I'M GOING TO GO FIND GALLUS. COMING?
NAH. I'M... I'M GONNA CHILL OUT HERE FOR A BIT.
OKAY—SEE YOU LATER!

THE COLISEUM OF FEATS.
WHEW! THANKS.
MY PLEASURE. WHAT ARE THESE FOR?
NO IDEA. IT BETTER NOT BE AS BIG A HASSLE AS GETTING IT INSTALLED WAS.
SO. SCHOOL OF FRIENDSHIP. KIND OF A BIG DEAL, HUH?
MY FATHER ENROLLED ME HERE BECAUSE HE HEARD ABOUT HOW INFLUENTIAL IT WAS AND WANTED ME TO...
...TO BECOME AN INFLUENCER MYSELF. IT'S KIND OF STRESSFUL, TO BE HONEST.
OH, BOY. I KNOW HOW THAT GOES.

MOST OF US CAME HERE BECAUSE OUR GROUP LEADERS WANTED US TO LEARN ABOUT FRIENDSHIP.
WE'RE ALL FOR IT NOW, BUT IT'S ROUGH BEING THE REPS FOR YOUR ENTIRE KIND.
AND NOW *THAT'S* BEING PUT TO THE TEST WITH THE FEATS. SHEESH.

ESPECIALLY SINCE THERE'S NOT MUCH PRECEDENT FOR GRIFFONS HAVING FRIENDLY RELATIONS WITH PONIES.
HA! NOPE. GUESS I'M STARTING A TREND. AND I GOTTA ADMIT, I REALLY LIKE IT.
HAHA! WOW! SUCH CONFIDENCE. I'M JEALOUS. NO WONDER YOU'RE THE LEADER.
HAHA— WHAT?

YOU'RE CLEARLY CARRYING THE GROUP. THE POISE, THE CHARISMA— EVERYONE SHOULD RESPECT YOUR AUTHORITY.

...YOU'RE RIGHT. THEY *SHOULD* LOOK UP TO ME.

THE STABLE RAPIDS.
WOW! YOU MAKE THAT LOOK EASY!
YONA STRONG! NO FEEL THE EXTRA WEIGHT!
AND YOU SPEAK THE LOCAL LANGUAGE SO WELL!
YONA IS QUICK STUDY.
AND I BET YOU CAN SNEAK ALL SORTS OF GOSSIP WITH YOUR FRIENDS WHEN YOU ALL SPEAK YAK.
YONA'S FRIENDS... DON'T SPEAK YAK. AT ALL.
REALLY? HOW ODD.
YOU WENT TO SO MUCH TROUBLE TO LEARN THEIR LANGUAGE, BUT THEY DIDN'T BOTHER TO LEARN YOURS?
I'M GOING TO CHECK IN ON THE OTHERS. DO YOU HAVE EVERYTHING UNDER CONTROL HERE?
Y-YEAH. YONA GOOD ON OWN.

SWEET APPLE ACRES.
I'M STARVING. WANT AN APPLE?
ARE WE ALLOWED TO?
I AIN'T ASKIN'. IF YOU DON'T TELL, I WON'T TELL.

THE FOOD AROUND HERE IS PRETTY GOOD. BUT WE DRAGONS USUALLY LIVE OFF GEMS.
THE SCHOOL MUST HAVE QUITE THE FOOD BUDGET.
HAHA—NAH, I EAT THE SAME STUFF AS EVERYONE ELSE.

WEIRD THAT THEY'D INVITE YOU TO THE SCHOOL, MAKE A BIG DEAL ABOUT INCLUDING YOU, BUT NOT SERVE WHAT YOU NEED TO EAT TO SURVIVE.
I'D HATE TO THINK HOW MUCH YOUR FRIENDS ARE SPENDING JUST TO GET YOU SNACKS.

CAN'T THINK OF A TIME THEY HAVE...

C'MON. I'M NOT HUNGRY ANYMORE.
WHATEVER YOU SAY!

BACK AT THE COLISEUM OF FEATS...
SHOULD I BE WORRIED WHAT THESE CAGES ARE FOR?
THEY DO SEEM CREEPY...
...BUT I'M SURE THE TEACHERS KNOW WHAT THEY'RE DOING.
YOU REALLY RESPECT THEM, DON'T YOU?
THEY'VE DONE A LOT FOR US CHANGELINGS.
I DON'T MEAN TO BE RUDE, BUT CAN YOU REALLY TURN INTO *ANYTHING?*
WELL... NO, BUT I CAN TAKE THE SHAPE OF A LOT OF THINGS!
BUT... YOU'RE STUCK IN THAT ONE FORM? YOU DON'T GET A MUSCLE CRAMP FROM THAT?

IT'S JUST—
SHAPE-CHANGING MAKES OTHERS NERVOUS.

SO... THE PONIES MAKE YOUR ENTIRE PEOPLE CHANGE THEIR WAY OF LIFE, THEN KEEP ONE SHAPE BECAUSE IT MAKES *THEM* UNCOMFORTABLE.
THAT SOUNDS LIKE ***DOMESTICATION*** MORE THAN FRIENDSHIP.
IT'S... IT'S NOT LIKE THAT...
WELL, EVEN IF IT WAS, AT LEAST YOUR ***FRIENDS*** AREN'T NERVOUS WHEN YOU CHANGE, RIGHT?

AT THE END OF THE DAY...
THIS HAS BEEN A PERFECT FIRST DAY, SANDBAR.
MM'GLAD...
YOU'RE QUITE BRAVE, YOU KNOW. MAKING FRIENDS WITH SO MANY FOREIGN CREATURES.
OH... NAW...
DO YOU THINK THEY APPRECIATE YOUR—OUR—CULTURE? I MEAN, REALLY?
MM-HMM...
...AND WHAT DO THE OTHER STUDENTS THINK? THE OTHER PONIES?
THEY'RE... Y'KNOW... FRIENDLY...

. . .

I'M STILL NEW TO TOWN. WALK ME TO THE INN?
O-OKAY!

YOU WANT TO SEE IF ANYPONY WANTS TO HANG OUT FIRST?
YES, OF COURSE.

HEY, DUDES! NOW THAT WE'RE DONE FOR THE DAY, YOU WANNA DO SOMETHING?

UH... GUYS?

Y'KNOW WHAT? IT'S BEEN A LONG DAY. YOU GUYS DO WHATEVER YOU WANT.

YEAH... BETTER REST UP FOR THE FEATS TOMORROW...

SURE. SEE IF I CAN GET SOMETHING DECENT TO EAT.

YAK YAKKITY YAK-YAK.

WHAT'S... WHAT'S GOING ON?

EVERYPONY'S JUST TIRED. YOU WERE WALKING ME BACK?
Y-YEAH, S-SURE!

Foal House
Come in & Hit the Hay
WOW... YOU'RE STAYING HERE? ALL THE OTHER STUDENTS STAY IN CAMPUS HOUSING.
I... DIDN'T REGISTER IN TIME.

I HAVEN'T EVEN HAD A CHANCE TO SEE THE TOWN. HOW ABOUT WE SKIP ON THE FEATS AND YOU GIVE ME A TOUR?
OH, MAN! I-I-I'D LOVE TO!

...BUT I CAN'T LEAVE MY FRIENDS HANGING. AND WE'RE ALL COUNTING ON YOU, TOO.

House
I UNDERSTAND. THEIR HAPPINESS COMES FIRST. GOOD NIGHT.
I... BUH... YUH...

MAYBE I DIDN'T *WANT* TO DO THE FEATS, HUH, SMOLDER...?

UGH... WHAT A DAY...

I CAN FINALLY PEEL THIS THING OFF...

I'M CALLING TO REPORT, FATHER.
I'M IN.

AMF!'19
Art By
Tony Fleecs

"WELCOME, ONE AND ALL, TO THE NEWEST FACILITY TO THE SCHOOL OF FRIENDSHIP—THE HIPPODROME!"
Feats of Friendship
I AM YOUR PRINCIPAL, AND THE PRINCESS OF FRIENDSHIP, TWILIGHT SPARKLE.
IT IS MY GREAT PLEASURE TO WELCOME YOU ALL TO THE FIRST EVER FEATS OF FRIENDSHIP!
YAAAAAAAAAAAAAAAAAAAAY
I KNOW WE HELPED SET THINGS UP, BUT...
IT'S A BIT DIFFERENT WHEN IT'S FILLED WITH A BAJILLION CHEERING PONIES.

SORRY-SORRY-SORRY! I MUST HAVE SLEPT IN! DID I MISS THE FIRST FEAT?
N-NO. PINKIE PIE'S OPENING CEREMONIES RAN LONG.

AND... EVERYONE IS HERE. SITTING TOGETHER.
WELL, YEAH. WE'RE ALL A TEAM.

SORRY IF WE WERE SNIPPY YESTERDAY. THE STRESS OF GETTING THINGS READY AND PERFORMING WAS GETTING TO ALL OF US, I THINK.

BUT WE'VE GOTTA SHAKE THAT OFF! PRINCIPAL TWILIGHT SAID SHE'S COUNTING ON US! TIME TO WIN AND PROVE WE'RE THE BEST!
WE'LL SEE ABOUT THAT.
CH'YEAH— 'CAUSE WE ARE!

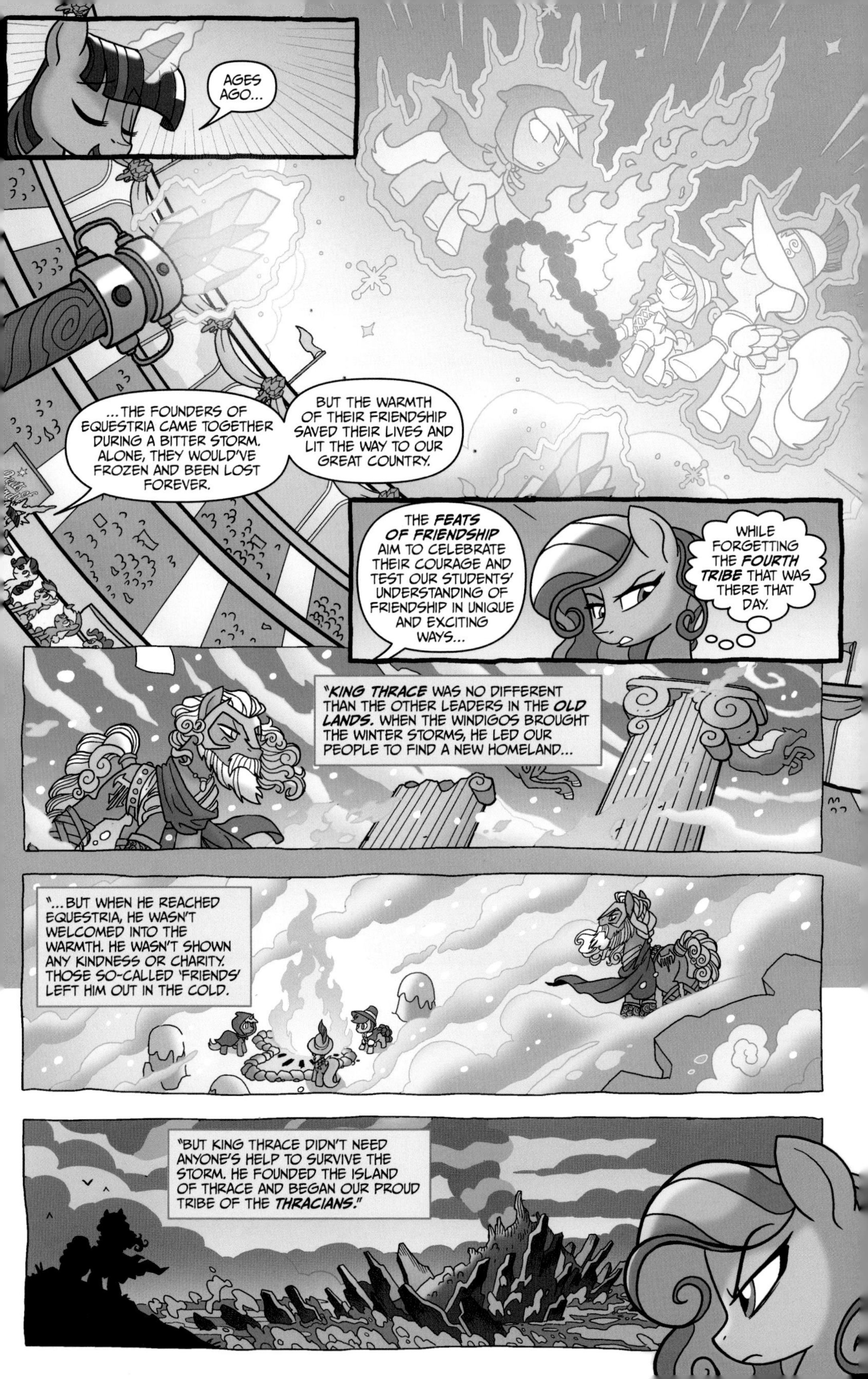
AGES AGO...
...THE FOUNDERS OF EQUESTRIA CAME TOGETHER DURING A BITTER STORM. ALONE, THEY WOULD'VE FROZEN AND BEEN LOST FOREVER.
BUT THE WARMTH OF THEIR FRIENDSHIP SAVED THEIR LIVES AND LIT THE WAY TO OUR GREAT COUNTRY.
THE FEATS OF FRIENDSHIP AIM TO CELEBRATE THEIR COURAGE AND TEST OUR STUDENTS' UNDERSTANDING OF FRIENDSHIP IN UNIQUE AND EXCITING WAYS...
WHILE FORGETTING THE FOURTH TRIBE THAT WAS THERE THAT DAY.
"KING THRACE WAS NO DIFFERENT THAN THE OTHER LEADERS IN THE OLD LANDS. WHEN THE WINDIGOS BROUGHT THE WINTER STORMS, HE LED OUR PEOPLE TO FIND A NEW HOMELAND...
"...BUT WHEN HE REACHED EQUESTRIA, HE WASN'T WELCOMED INTO THE WARMTH. HE WASN'T SHOWN ANY KINDNESS OR CHARITY. THOSE SO-CALLED 'FRIENDS' LEFT HIM OUT IN THE COLD.
"BUT KING THRACE DIDN'T NEED ANYONE'S HELP TO SURVIVE THE STORM. HE FOUNDED THE ISLAND OF THRACE AND BEGAN OUR PROUD TRIBE OF THE THRACIANS."

...IN RETROSPECT, HE WASN'T VERY CREATIVE AT NAMING THINGS.
BUT THAT'S BESIDE THE POINT! WE WERE LEFT BEHIND, FORGOTTEN, WHILE THE REST OF THE PONIES BECAME INFECTED WITH THAT VILE LIE THAT IS "FRIENDSHIP"...
WE DON'T WANT IT ANYMORE, ANYWAY. IT'S A WEAKNESS. AND WE'LL EXPOSE IT BY DESTROYING IT.

YO! SWIFT FOOT!
BUH!
YOU'VE BEEN OFF IN YOUR OWN LITTLE WORLD THE WHOLE WAY HERE. LISTEN UP! PROFESSOR APPLEJACK IS EXPLAINING THE RULES.

...WITH THE MOST APPLES WINS. IT AIN'T GONNA BE EASY, THOUGH.
FRIENDSHIP COMES FROM CLEAR **COMMUNICATION.**
LISTEN TO EACH OTHER AND COORDINATE, Y'HEAR?

HERE'S THE PLAN! EVERYONE WHO CAN FLY WILL DROP APPLES DOWN INTO THE BASKETS.
THE REST OF YOU HAUL THEM TO THE THE DROP SITES. COOL? COOL! **GO!**

I'VE GOT TO FOCUS! THEY'RE GOING TO BE TOO COORDINATED AT THIS RATE. HOW DO I...?
HMM-HMM-HMM!

YONA! TWO BASKETS?
YUP! YONA STRONGEST ONE, SO CAN CARRY MORE!

I'M GLAD YOU ARE! OTHERWISE I'D FEEL BAD YOUR FRIENDS GAVE ME THIS HANDY CART INSTEAD OF YOU.
CART... WOULD BE NICE...

HEY! WHERE ARE YOU GOING?!
YAK YAKKITY YAK.

HRRGH! SANDBAR! CAN YOU HELP ME OUT!
WE AREN'T GONNA HAUL MUCH IF WE GO TWO TO A WAGON.

I KNOW, BUT IF I HAD SOMEONE STRONG WITH ME, MAYBE WE COULD GO FASTER...
W-WHEN YOU PUT IT THAT WAY...!

BARK BARK
...WHAT'S THAT SOUND?

BARK BARK
WHOA-HO-HO! LOOK AT ALL THOSE ORTHOS HOUNDS!
NYAGH!
NO NO ABSOLUTELY NOT NO!
THAT'S THE SPIRIT!

TEAM Y-6

AW! BUMMER!

FORGET IT! JUST KEEP THEM OUT OF THE BARN!

TEAM
LOOK HOW MUCH SWIFT FOOT HAULED IN!

GOOD THING THE PRINCIPAL ASSIGNED HER TO OUR TEAM. OTHERWISE WE'D BARELY HAVE ANY APPLES.
I MEAN... I ***TRIED.*** HER NAME IS "***SWIFT***
FOOT" FOR CRYIN' OUT LOUD...

LATER—AT THE STABLE RAPIDS...
THE SECOND FEAT IS TO CROSS THE RIVER!
WE'LL GRADE YA ON YOUR BRIDGE'S STABILITY AND COMPLETION!
BRIDGES ARE LIKE FRIENDSHIPS—YOU WON'T GET FAR WITHOUT BEING GENEROUS WITH ONE ANOTHER! HINT-HINT!
HAHAHA!
OKAY... THOSE OF US WITH HANDS SHOULD DEAL WITH THE CONSTRUCTION. EVERYONE ELSE CAN HELP ORGANIZE SUPPLIES.
ISN'T IT JUST GREAT THAT GALLUS TOOK IT UPON HIMSELF TO BE OUR GROUP LEADER?
NOT REALLY.
OOH! OOH! I CAN FLY AND SWIM! WHAT IF I START BUILDING FROM THE OTHER BANK?
YEAH! I BET YOU'LL WORK FASTER ON YOUR OWN!
HEY! WE NEED THAT!
SOME OF US HAVE IDEAS TOO, Y'KNOW!

WE *HAVE* TO WIN THIS! THE PRINCIPAL SAID WE'RE REPRESENTING *EVERYTHING!* WHAT ARE YOU DOING?!

NOT MUCH. WE DON'T HAVE ANY NAILS.
HOW ARE WE SUPPOSED TO BUILD A BRIDGE WITHOUT NAILS?!

HEY! DOES YOUR TEAM'S BIN HAVE ANY ANCHOR ROPES?
HUH? YEAH, LOADS OF THEM. DO YOU HAVE ANY NAILS?

NO, BUT WE'VE GOT TONS OF WOOD GLUE. TEAM B-4 HAS BUNCHES OF NAILS, AND TEAM R-8 SEEMS TO HAVE MORE TOOLS THAN THEY CAN HANDLE.

THAT'S IT. THAT'S THE TRICK. GENEROSITY.
NO ONE TEAM CAN BUILD A BRIDGE WITH WHAT THEY'VE GOT. WE ALL HAVE TO COME TOGETHER TO BUILD ONE BRIDGE.
IF WE ALL SHARE, EVERYONE WINS.

OR, Y'KNOW, EVERYONE CAN LISTEN TO THE NEW GIRL.

HERE'S ONE FOR THE FAR BANK!

WHAT'S WITH YOU?
SILVERSTREAM CHANGES FORMS AND NOBODY CARES.
YEAH? THAT'S WHAT HIPPOGRIFF-SEAPONIES DO.
IT'S WHAT CHANGELINGS DO, TOO.

WELL... THE RESULTS CERTAINLY ARE...
AWFUL.
...I WAS GOING TO SAY "RUSTIC."

TEAMS Y-6 AND R-8 BUILT THE CLOSEST THING TO A BRIDGE, BUT NOBODY UNDERSTOOD THE POINT OF THE FEAT.
SO WE'LL TOSS THEM SOME PITY POINTS, BUT I'M NOT REWARDING THEM FOR MESSING UP.

BAD NEWS, GUYS. WE DIDN'T SCORE VERY WELL. I GUESS OUR FRIENDSHIP ISN'T STRONG ENOUGH.

WE'RE NOT GOING TO WIN AT THIS RATE.
PRINCIPAL TWILIGHT IS COUNTING ON US...

C'MON, GUYS! WE'VE GOT TO GET IT TOGETHER! EVERYONE IS EXPECTING US TO PULL THIS OFF!
WELL, MAYBE IF EVERYONE HAD *LISTENED* TO ME...

WHO DIED AND MADE YOU LEADER?!
I'M SORRY! WHEN DID WE NEED TO VOTE ON IDEAS?!

YAKKITY YIK-YAK.
EXACTLY.
SORRY? I DON'T UNDERSTAND.

STOP FIGHTING! IT'S ALMOST OUR TURN FOR THE THIRD FEAT! WE'RE SETTING A BAD EXAMPLE FOR OUR NEW FRIEND!

DON'T WORRY ABOUT ME, OCELLUS. I'M JUST ***FINE.***

RRRRUMBLE
THE THIRD FEAT IS ALL ABOUT **COOPERATION.** BY WORKING TOGETHER, FRIENDS CAN ACCOMPLISH ANYTHING. EACH TEAM HAS TO LOOK OUT FOR EACH OTHER WHILE CAGING THE DANGEROUS BEAST.
Feats of Friendship
HUGE THANKS TO THE ADMINISTRATORS OF TARTARUS FOR LOANING US TODAY'S CHALLENGE!
THE TRIPLE THREAT FOR THE PRICE OF ONE!
THE SCARIEST SISTERS ANYWHERE!
CHIMERA!!!
WHAT?!

FASSSSTER, LITTLE ONE! WE'RE RIGHT BEHIND YOU!

CLANG

TOO EASY!

ONE DOWN! SSSSIX TO GO!

WHAT ARE WE GONNA DO?!
OH, *NOW* YOU WANT MY INPUT?

DO NOT START WITH ME RIGHT NOW!

THE YAK IS THE STRONGEST ONE. CAGE HER NEXT.
CLLANG

WE'RE TWO DOWN! WE NEED A PLAN, DUDES!
OKAY... OKAY... OKAY...

OKAY!
SMOLDER! SILVERSTREAM! PICK A HEAD!
WE'LL KEEP HER—THEM?—DISTRACTED!

SANDBAR! YONA! START PUSHING HER TOWARDS THE BIG CAGE!
BOGUS...

AH-AH-AH! SSSAW YOU COMING!

RRRGH! YONA DRAG CHIMERA INTO CAGE! SANDBAR! COME! HELP!
I... UM...

I'LL GET HELP!
YAK YAKKING YAK!
WHOA! LANGUAGE!

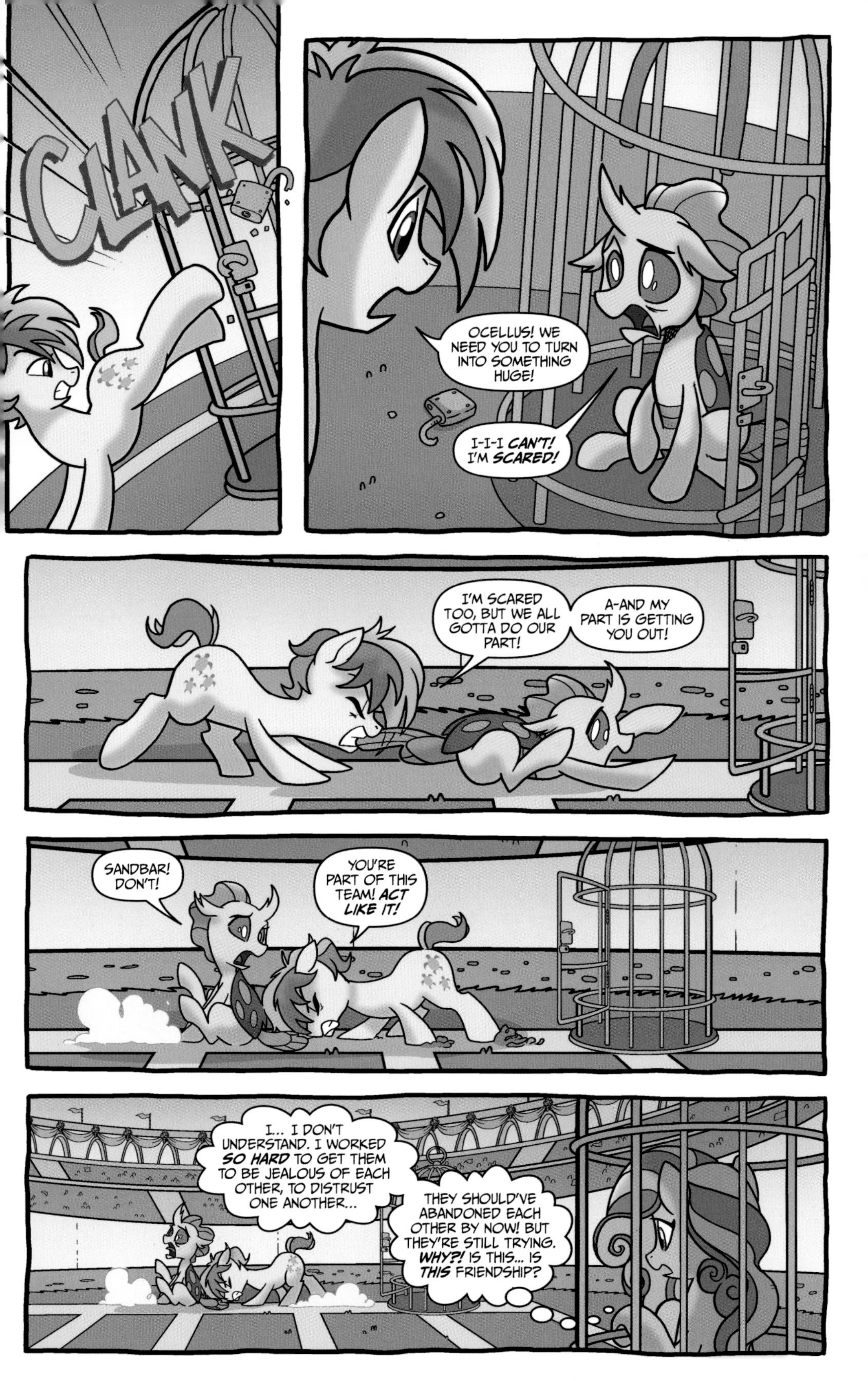
CLANK
OCELLUS! WE NEED YOU TO TURN INTO SOMETHING HUGE!
I-I-I CAN'T! I'M SCARED!
I'M SCARED TOO, BUT WE ALL GOTTA DO OUR PART!
A-AND MY PART IS GETTING YOU OUT!
SANDBAR! DON'T!
YOU'RE PART OF THIS TEAM! ACT LIKE IT!
I... I DON'T UNDERSTAND. I WORKED SO HARD TO GET THEM TO BE JEALOUS OF EACH OTHER, TO DISTRUST ONE ANOTHER...
THEY SHOULD'VE ABANDONED EACH OTHER BY NOW! BUT THEY'RE STILL TRYING. WHY?! IS THIS... IS THIS FRIENDSHIP?

FINE.

AAAHHHHHH!

AAAHHHHHHH!

SLAM!

AAAAAAAND TIME! THAT WAS AWESOME!
YAY!
THAT... THAT WAS TRULY AMAZING! THE WAY YOU ALL WORKED TOGETHER WAS...
BULLYING IS NOT TEAMWORK!

OCELLUS STEAL ALL THE GLORY! YONA HAD IT! YAKKING YAKKITY YAK!
SANDBAR MADE ME...

WE. DON'T. SPEAK. YAK!
YAK-YAKKA-YAK!

WE DIDN'T WIN THAT. WE JUST FAILED AT FAILING IT.
IS IT REALLY THAT HARD TO ADMIT I SAVED THE DAY?
YEAH! IF YOUR EGO GETS ANY BIGGER, IT'LL SUFFOCATE US!
MY EGO?! WHAT ABOUT YOU?!
THIS IS IT... I DID IT!
EQUESTRIA'S SYMBOL OF CROSS-SPECIES HARMONY IS FALLING APART!

Art By
Tony Fleecs
AMF! 19

THE HIPPODROME, JUST OUTSIDE THE SCHOOL OF FRIENDSHIP.
...CAN'T STAND YOU WHEN...!
...ACTING LIKE A TOTAL JERK...!
...I CAN'T BELIEVE YOU...!
...WHEN I'M TRYING TO...!
THIS... THIS IS IT! MY TEAM IS IMPLODING! THEIR FRIENDSHIPS ARE RUINED!
IT'S... JUST LIKE I WANTED... RIGHT?
IT'S CERTAINLY WHAT I WAS SENT HERE TO DO...

THE KINGDOM OF THRACE, DAYS AGO...
YOU'RE IN TROUBLE NOW, LITTLE SISTER!
WH-WHAT? WHAT DID I DO?

DUNNO. DAD SAID HE WANTED TO SEE YOU, SO THAT *CAN'T* BE GOOD.
HE SENT US A WHILE AGO, BUT WE TOOK OUR TIME FINDING YOU. HURRY-HURRY!

B-BLONN DI! *YOU* MADE ME LATE!
IT'S *OUR* WORD AGAINST YOURS, BRAT.

SHINING LIGHT?
WHAT? IT'S YOUR FAULT FOR BEING SO EASY TO PICK ON.

YOU TWO ARE THE WORST!

I'M SORRY, FATHER! I CAME AS SOON AS THEY TOLD ME—
SAVE YOUR EXCUSES, GIRL. YOU HAVE WORK TO DO.

TERRI BELLE. YOUR REPORT.
YES, FATHER.
PRINCESS TWILIGHT SPARKLE HAS ANNOUNCED A CONTEST TO DISPLAY THE MERITS OF FRIENDSHIP. NOT JUST BETWEEN PONIES, BUT ACROSS SPECIES.

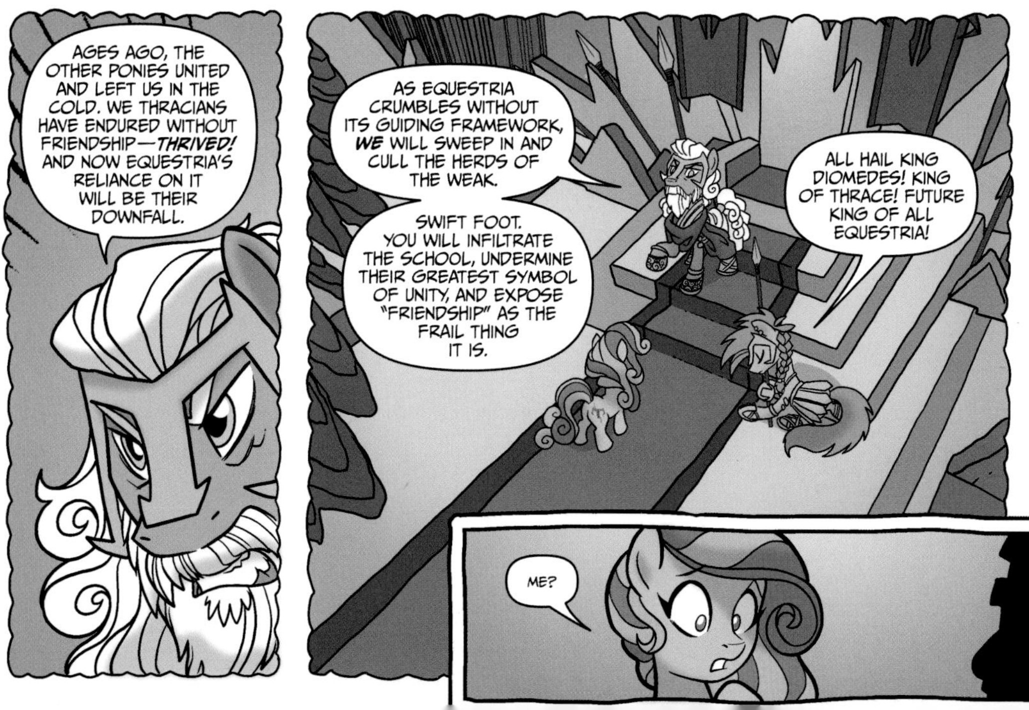
AGES AGO, THE OTHER PONIES UNITED AND LEFT US IN THE COLD. WE THRACIANS HAVE ENDURED WITHOUT FRIENDSHIP—***THRIVED!*** AND NOW EQUESTRIA'S RELIANCE ON IT WILL BE THEIR DOWNFALL.
AS EQUESTRIA CRUMBLES WITHOUT ITS GUIDING FRAMEWORK, ***WE*** WILL SWEEP IN AND CULL THE HERDS OF THE WEAK.
SWIFT FOOT. YOU WILL INFILTRATE THE SCHOOL, UNDERMINE THEIR GREATEST SYMBOL OF UNITY, AND EXPOSE "FRIENDSHIP" AS THE FRAIL THING IT IS.
ALL HAIL KING DIOMEDES! KING OF THRACE! FUTURE KING OF ALL EQUESTRIA!
ME?

ARE YOU *REFUSING?*
NO-NO-NO! ***NEVER,*** FATHER! J-JUST... WHY NOT SEND TERRI BELLE? SHE'S SMARTER AND CRAFTIER THAN I AM!
TRUE, BUT I'M TOO OLD TO PLAY THE PART.
AND THE TWINS ARE USELESS FOR ANYTHING THAT REQUIRES TACT.
I'VE COMPILED ALL THE PERTINENT INTEL YOU'LL NEED. THE STUDENTS TO GET CLOSE TO, THEIR IMPORTANCE TO THEIR KIND, AND THE TENSIONS BETWEEN RACES.
ALL YOU HAVE TO DO IS GET IN CLOSE AND TURN THEM AGAINST EACH OTHER.
TH-THANK YOU, SISTER. B-BUT ***HOW*** DO I GET IN CLOSE?
SIMPLE. YOU BECOME THEIR "FRIEND."
YOU MAKE IT SOUND SO EASY.
ONCE YOU KNOW HOW TO EXPLOIT IT— *IT IS.*
I WILL STUDY THIS AND EMBARK AS SOON AS POSSIBLE. I'LL EXPOSE THESE FRAUDS AND PAVE THE WAY TO YOUR GLORIOUS CONQUEST.
EXCELLENT. MAKE ME PROUD, SWIFT FOOT.

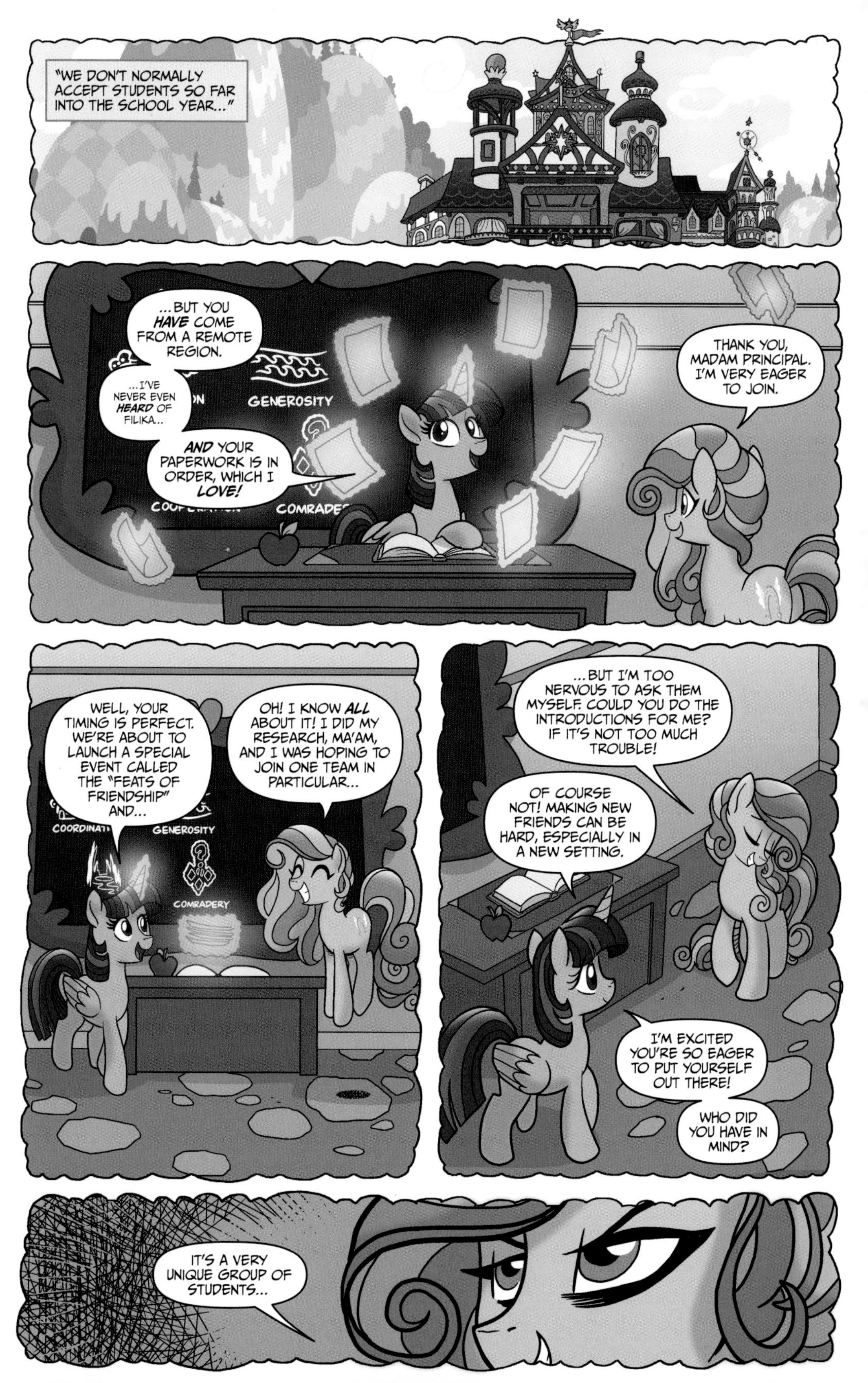
"WE DON'T NORMALLY ACCEPT STUDENTS SO FAR INTO THE SCHOOL YEAR..."
...BUT YOU HAVE COME FROM A REMOTE REGION.
...I'VE NEVER EVEN HEARD OF FILIKA...
AND YOUR PAPERWORK IS IN ORDER, WHICH I LOVE!
GENEROSITY
COMRADES
THANK YOU, MADAM PRINCIPAL. I'M VERY EAGER TO JOIN.
WELL, YOUR TIMING IS PERFECT. WE'RE ABOUT TO LAUNCH A SPECIAL EVENT CALLED THE "FEATS OF FRIENDSHIP" AND...
OH! I KNOW ALL ABOUT IT! I DID MY RESEARCH, MA'AM, AND I WAS HOPING TO JOIN ONE TEAM IN PARTICULAR...
GENEROSITY
COMRADERY
...BUT I'M TOO NERVOUS TO ASK THEM MYSELF. COULD YOU DO THE INTRODUCTIONS FOR ME? IF IT'S NOT TOO MUCH TROUBLE!
OF COURSE NOT! MAKING NEW FRIENDS CAN BE HARD, ESPECIALLY IN A NEW SETTING.
I'M EXCITED YOU'RE SO EAGER TO PUT YOURSELF OUT THERE!
WHO DID YOU HAVE IN MIND?
IT'S A VERY UNIQUE GROUP OF STUDENTS...

IT'S BEEN... DIFFICULT. THE ALLURE OF FRIENDSHIP IS STRONG. THESE PERFECT STRANGERS ACCEPTED ME...
TREATED ME WITH MORE KINDNESS THAN MY OWN FAMILY...

BUT IT *IS* A LIE. I'VE ONLY BEEN HERE A SHORT TIME, AND WITH BARELY ANY EFFORT, I'VE PITTED THEM AGAINST EACH OTHER.
SO MUCH FOR THE "MAGIC OF FRIENDSHIP."

...SO WHY EVEN **ACT** LIKE YOU WANT YONA AROUND?!
I... WE... YOU...!
YEK YOKKITY YAK YORK!

PFFFFT! **WHAT?**

I WAS TRYING TO SAY, "WE DO CARE AND WE'RE TRYING" IN YAK.
HAW! YOU ARE SAYING, "WE NEED MORE MAYO FOR THE TROUT BIKE!"

WAIT. YOU ARE KNOWING HOW TO SPEAK YAK?
NO. THAT'S THE PROBLEM!
WE'VE BEEN TRYING TO LEARN IT SO YOU'D FEEL MORE AT HOME.
ALL OF YOU?!

YEAH. BUT, LIKE, YOUR LANGUAGE IS REALLY HARD.
AND IN BETWEEN ALL OUR OTHER LESSONS, WE HAVEN'T HAD TIME TO REALLY STUDY IT.

BUT... WHY NOT ASK YONA TO HELP?
WE WANTED TO SURPRISE YOU. AND WE DIDN'T WANT TO INSULT YOU BY BUTCHERING IT.
I MEAN, YOU ALREADY SPEAK OURS FLUENTLY.
SORTA.

YONA THOUGHT SHE HAD WORST FRIENDS WHO IGNORE WHO YONA IS!
YONA HAS BEST FRIENDS WHO TRY HARD FOR YONA!

YONA IS SORRY FOR YELLING! YOU DID NOT MEAN TO STEAL YONA'S THUNDER, RIGHT?
R-RIGHT. I ONLY CHARGED THE CHIMERA BECAUSE SANDBAR MADE ME.

YEAH... THAT WAS TOTALLY NOT COOL OF ME. I LOST MY MELLOW. I'M *REALLY* SORRY, OCELLUS.
IT *WAS* PRETTY RUDE, BUT...

...I'M NO BETTER. I'VE BEEN *REALLY* JEALOUS OF YOU LATELY, SILVERSTREAM. AND THAT'S RUDE.
JEALOUS? OF *ME?* WHY?!

BECAUSE YOU CAN CHANGE FORM IN FRONT OF EVERYONE AND NOBODY MINDS. BUT IF *I* CHANGE, PEOPLE GET SCARED...

AWW! I'M *SO* SORRY! I NEVER THOUGHT ABOUT IT THAT WAY! WE SHAPE-CHANGERS NEED TO LOOK OUT FOR EACH OTHER!

NO, WE ALL NEED TO LOOK AFTER EACH OTHER. IF SOMEBODY HAS A PROBLEM WITH WHO YOU ARE, THEN THEY HAVE TO TAKE IT UP WITH ALL OF US!
YONA WILL SQUISH THEM INTO JELLY!
YEAH!

TH-THAT'S NOT NECESSARY...
W-WE CAN JUST TALK TO THE TEACHERS!

THAT GOES FOR ALL OF YOU. ≥SIGH≤ AND I'VE DONE A BAD JOB OF SHOWING IT.
I'M SORRY. I'VE BEEN A JERK LATELY.
YEAH, YOU HAVE!

AND I HAVEN'T BEEN GREAT EITHER. SO I'M SORRY, TOO.
A DRAGON? APOLOGIZING?
YEAH-YEAH-YEAH.

THIS IS STUPID! THE FEATS ARE SUPPOSED TO SHOW OFF OUR FRIENDSHIP, NOT TEAR IT APART!
THE STRESS HAS BEEN MAKING ME MOLT.

PLUS TRYING TO MAKE THE PRINCIPAL PROUD. PLUS REPRESENTING OUR PEOPLE. TRYING TO IMPRESS EVERYONE...
YEAH...

...EVERYONE...

WINNING THIS THING ISN'T WORTH LOSING OUR FRIENDSHIP. WHAT DO YA SAY, GUYS? STILL FRIENDS?
YEAH!

≷AHEM≶ SORRY YOU HAD TO SEE ALL THAT. WE AREN'T USUALLY LIKE THIS.
YOU'RE STILL FRIENDS... JUST LIKE THAT?

WE... HAVE A LOT TO TALK ABOUT. BUT YEAH. FRIENDSHIP IS HARD WORK.
AND, LIKE, REALLY MESSY SOMETIMES.

BUT WITH A HEALTHY DOSE OF FORGIVENESS AND COMMUNICATION, YOU CAN MAKE IT WORK! BECAUSE IT'S *TOTALLY* WORTH IT!
WHAT YOU SAID! HAHA!
YAK YAKKITY YAK-YAK!

WAIT... WAS THAT THE LESSON THE FEATS OF FRIENDSHIP WAS TRYING TO TEACH US ALL ALONG? UGH!
OH NO! WE'RE ***LEARNING!***

AND... I GUESS WHILE WE'RE AT IT... UM...
SORRY FOR GETTING JEALOUS ABOUT GETTING YOUR ATTENTION...
ARE YOU ***SERIOUS?***

OF COURSE. YOU'RE THE COOL NEW EXCHANGE STUDENT. I GUESS WE WERE ALL TRYING TO IMPRESS YOU, TOO.
WHAT DO YOU SAY? STILL WANT TO HANG WITH US?

YOU... YOU'D ALL STILL BE FRIENDS WITH ME? AFTER EVERYTHING I'VE DONE?

HAHA—WHAT? YOU'VE SHOWN US NOTHING BUT COMPASSION AND CONCERN FOR US AND OUR CULTURES.
NOTHING WRONG WITH BEING AWESOME.

I... HAVEN'T...

OKAY. THANK YOU.

WE'RE ABOUT TO START THE FINAL FEAT.
YONA IS READY FOR ANYTHING NOW!
LET'S DO OUR BEST, BUT MORE IMPORTANTLY, LET'S DO IT TOGETHER!
ON THREE!
ONE!
TWO!
THREE!
GO TEAM!!!

OUR STUDENTS HAVE DONE AN EXCELLENT JOB OF SHOWING US THE STRENGTHS OF THEIR FRIENDSHIPS, AND WHAT HAPPENS WHEN WE LET THAT STRENGTH LAPSE.
FOR OUR FINAL FEAT, WE'LL BE SHOWCASING THEIR COMRADERY!
THROUGH THICK AND THIN, THE GOOD TIMES AND THE BAD, THE STRONGEST OF FRIENDSHIPS WILL SEE YOU THROUGH ANYTHING! GOOD FRIENDS CAN BE LIKE A SECOND FAMILY.
SO, STUDENTS, CAN YOU STICK TOGETHER AND TAKE DOWN—
Feats of Friendship

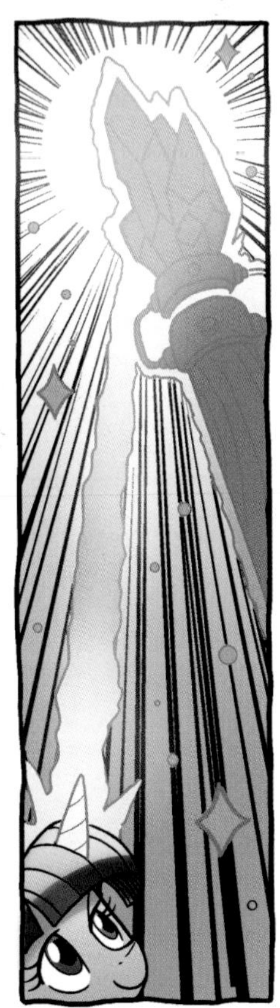

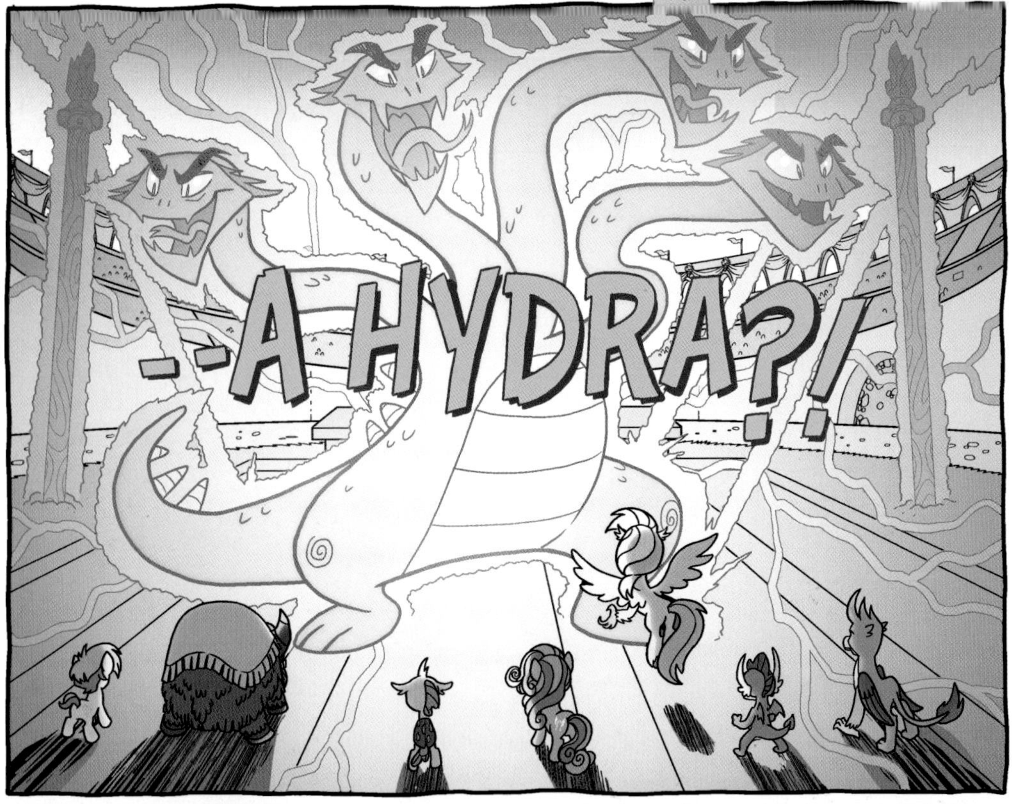
...A HYDRA?!

WHAT'S THE PLAN, GALLUS?
THAT ONE ON THE LEFT LOOKS LIKE MY UNCLE.

PAIR OFF AND PICK A HEAD!

OCELLUS!
I KNOW! IT'S JUST AN ILLUSION!
RIGHT! SHOW 'EM WHAT A **REAL** HYDRA SHOULD LOOK LIKE!

WOO! DOWN FOR THE COUNT!
POOF!
Friend
AND TEAM Y-6 FINISHES IN RECORD TIME! THAT WAS *AMAZING!*

WE.
ARE.
EPIC.
HAHA— OH MAN, I'M GLAD THAT WORKED...

THAT WAS AMAZING! *YOU* WERE AMAZING!

IS THAT ALL? SEND YONA ANOTHER!

I'M GLAD YOU WERE HERE WITH US FOR THIS MOMENT.

I AM, TOO.

AND SO...
THIS ISN'T RIGHT. SWIFT FOOT SHOULD BE HERE WITH US.
PINKIE PIE DELAYED THE CLOSING CEREMONIES FOR AS LONG AS SHE COULD.
1
2
3
SHE'S HAD A REALLY EXHAUSTING FEW DAYS. MAYBE SHE WENT BACK TO THE INN TO REST? WE'LL BRING HER MEDAL TO HER LATER.
Y-YEAH. S-SHE WOULDN'T LEAVE W-WITHOUT SAYING GOODBYE...
I WISH I WAS DOWN THERE WITH YOU ALL. IT... HURTS TO BE APART.
BUT YOU ALL EARNED THIS MOMENT...
...AND I HAVEN'T.

FAREWELL, EQUESTRIA. GOODBYE, MY... FRIENDS.
YOUR FRIENDSHIP TRULY IS MAGIC.
I'LL RETURN TO THRACE. TRY TO CONVINCE THEM OF YOUR STRENGTH. MAYBE EVEN THAT FRIENDSHIP IS WORTH EXPLORING...
AND IF NOT...
...I WILL FIGHT TO PROTECT MY FRIENDS.
The End!

Art By
JustaSuta

Art By
JustaSuta

Art By
JustaSuta

Art By
Katie O'Neill

Art By
Katie O'Neill

Art By
Katie O'Neill

E M M K G J F A K R F Q G G S P U D C B

N W T H R A C E B X C P H H N N F V O Y

C O M R A D E R Y E E Q U E H H I T O F

F P Y Y R B O T T N H G N A Y Q S H P M

A P I H S D N E I R F Z A E E M B E E S

Q Y S N O M F I W Q P J P H N Y J J R M

O K G E W T R F J N I D I Z R V T G A S

J P M C G K C D B M R X S M N L R O T B

G C R Z G Z M D V F I X V M L R Y S I L

D V U F K J D M I L O Y Q V R W P U O S

T N P G J S U M J T T T F A W I M T N S

X P J K E D E S W I F T F O O T P O W R

Y N O I T A N I D R O O C J T F V E A X

E F M D S W J D S B A F B N R I E E H G

Z S T A E F X M R B E O X Y C R G S X L

R W K P T J C P E U C F X F Y V T M L C

M O U H S M G B B S Q R D V J G J W U F

V C M G E N E R O S I T Y C B B R C A S

P L Q O V L O J Z Q J D C K U C C W S D

H F Y M U U K A Q E L G E Q M Q R P K I

WORD LIST:

COMRADERY
COOPERATION
COORDINATION
FEATS
FRIENDSHIP
GENEROSITY
SWIFT FOOT
THRACE

WILL YOU HELP ME FIND THESE WORDS?